Praise f

'Utterly enchanting'
Jill Mansell

'Magic sparkles from every page'
Miranda Dickinson

'Young, fab and incredibly talented. I think I
manage to keep my massive jealousy of Carrie
Hope Fletcher just about under control :-)'
Jenny Colgan

'A magical treat'
Heat

'Romantic'
Daily Mail

'Reminded me so much of Cecelia Ahern'
Ali McNamara

'A beautifully written love story,
full of hope, heart and happy ever after'
Jo Thomas

Also by Carrie Hope Fletcher

All I Know Now
On the Other Side

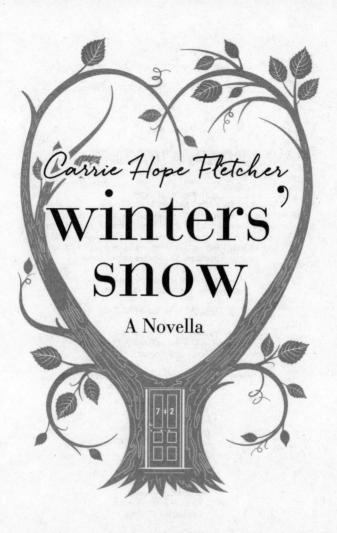

Carrie Hope Fletcher

winters' snow

A Novella

7 + 2

sphere

SPHERE

First published in Great Britain in 2016 by Sphere

A CIP catalogue record for this book is
available from the British Library.

ISBN 978-0-7515-6870-7

Typeset in Sabon by M Rules
Printed and bound in Great Britain by
Clays Ltd, Elcograf S.p.A.

Papers used by Sphere are from well-managed forests
and other responsible sources.

MIX
Paper from
responsible sources
FSC® C104740

Sphere
An imprint of
Little, Brown Book Group
Carmelite House
50 Victoria Embankment
London EC4Y 0DZ

An Hachette UK Company
www.hachette.co.uk

www.littlebrown.co.uk

1

Fight

Vincent Winters was dead. Aged eighty-three he had keeled over after eating some questionable, possibly poisonous fruit from a tree his lost love had planted years before. The street Vincent now found himself on was one he'd not visited in a very long time but it was exactly as he remembered. All the houses stood unchanged. The cherry blossom trees that lined the kerb were lying almost flat against the pavement, in an impossible fight to stay upright in the strange gale that Vincent also found himself leaning into. The wind howled like a thousand wolves, drowning out any chance of calling for help, or hearing it should help even arrive. One moment he had been in Jim Summer's garden and then, after just one bite of the forbidden fruit, he had suddenly found himself pushing against these ferocious winds. What made it a thousand times worse was that he knew exactly where he was and could see the place he'd wanted to go back to ever since the moment he'd last left it, all those years ago. At the end of the road was the apartment building where he'd spent the happiest days of his life – not a hundred yards away he could see Evie Snow's balcony. His only wish was to get back to that apartment, that balcony, but fighting against the gale, with one foot unsteadily shuffling in front of the other, he was barely moving. Vincent didn't know how long he'd been hunched forwards, his hands aching from holding his black coat tightly around his neck and his eyes streaming from the cold. It could have been for ever.

One thing Vincent did know was that he was younger. He felt it in his bones. He may have died at eighty-three but now his knees didn't creak, his back didn't ache and he still had all his teeth. He didn't need a mirror to know his hair was black instead of grey because he could see it, long and shaggy, blowing about his face. He was twenty-eight once more, he was sure of it. Twenty-eight isn't a special age for most. There are no special greeting cards for being a year closer to thirty. And yet twenty-eight had always been special to him because that was when he had met Evie.

Evie Snow had been the love of his life and every lifetime he would ever live, he believed – but they had never got the ending they wanted. Vincent couldn't offer her security or the guarantee life would always be OK. He could only offer Evie love and freedom. In theory that had been enough for Evie, but in reality the need for her mother's approval and fear for her brother's future if she was disowned by her parents outweighed her own happiness. Vincent hadn't understood it nor believed it was the right thing to do but he had respected her decision, walked away and let her marry someone else. The only consolation being that Vincent knew that the someone else was Jim Summer. Jim was Evie's oldest friend, the epitome of a gentleman, and he had loved Evie since they were children. Vincent knew she had been well looked after.

Just the thought of Evie made him eager to push forwards, to find her and tell her all the things he'd regretted not saying ever since he left her that fateful day, but the gale was still fierce around him. *Maybe I should stop to rest for just a moment*, he thought. As soon as the weight shifted back from the balls of his feet the wind ceased, the cherry trees stood tall again and an eerie silence followed in its wake. In the quiet and the calm, Vincent noticed the pumpkins on the doorsteps of the pastel-painted houses and he saw that the trees had lost all of their leaves.

Halloween, he thought, *Evie's birthday.*

As soon as his body tilted, even just a little, towards Evie's flat, the wind began once more. It roared louder and blew harder even than before but when Vincent stumbled backwards it ended as abruptly as it had started. Puzzled, Vincent took another step backwards. Nothing. No hurricane, just quiet. Vincent took a step to the side and again, nothing. To the other side, nothing. Then Vincent pressed a toe just an inch in front of him and held it to the surface of the road and the wind blew. He lifted his foot, it stopped, and he understood. If he was to make any progress towards Evie, he was going to have to fight against a seemingly unstoppable force. With that realisation, a breeze brushed the leaves that had been huddled against the kerbside and stirred them up into a frenzy. They lifted, floated and tumbled in the air around Vincent, dancing an autumnal ballet, brushing against his stubbled cheeks and ruffling his shaggy hair. They twirled and twisted until together they settled calmly in front of Vincent's black boots in a peculiar arrangement. Vincent looked closely and noticed they had formed words.

Prove yourself worthy.
Prove yourself true.
Fight like you didn't
and she'll come to you.

'Fight ...' Vincent muttered. He wanted to pretend he didn't know what the message meant but he knew and he couldn't ignore it any more. After Vincent had left Evie, one thought had always plagued him.

I didn't fight hard enough for her.

That thought had balled itself up and turned itself into a stone which had resided inside his heart. Every year it grew: it turned into a rock, and then a brick, until after fifty-five years, it was an anvil and he'd carried its burden. It had kept him from sleeping and haunted his dreams when he did finally drift, and even though he'd eventually found someone to share his life with, his mind was always dragged back to memories

5

of green coats, geese and hard boiled sweets. Vincent's heavy heart had always longed for Evie Snow.

'You have to fight for her, Vincent.'

Vincent's head snapped up and he was greeted by a vaguely familiar smile. The portly man in front of him was shorter than Vincent by a good foot and a few inches but his heart radiated warmth and Vincent welcomed it after the blistering cold of the wind. The man was slightly balding and his weathered skin made him look much older than his real age of forty-six.

'You ... you're Lieffe, right?' said Vincent, holding out his hand for Lieffe to shake.

'I am.' Lieffe bobbed his head, shaking Vincent's outstretched hand. Although they'd only met once in life, Lieffe was so pleased Vincent had remembered him.

'I have to say, I'm glad to see a friendly face.' Vincent looked out from behind his hair. 'I'm not entirely sure what's going on.'

'Well first things first. You know you're dead, right?' Lieffe raised a furry grey eyebrow.

'Tactful.' Vincent laughed. 'Yes. I remember my death *vividly*,' he said, recalling hearing Evie's voice whisper his name as all hell was breaking loose around him after he'd bitten into the fruit.

'*Wonderful!* Sometimes it takes so long to convince

people their lives are over. It's rather dull.' Lieffe put an arm around Vincent (it would have been around his shoulders if Lieffe could have reached them) and guided him away from Evie's flat. 'Secondly, the reason you're here is because something is stopping you from moving on.' They'd reached the end of the street and Lieffe abruptly stopped walking and turned to face him. 'You're holding onto something that you need to let go of. Do you have any idea what that may be?' Lieffe's eyes glistened as Vincent tried to avoid his gaze. 'It could be one thing or … maybe a few?' Lieffe said, his eyes flicking back to Evie's flat for just a moment.

Vincent nodded. *No point in hiding it*, he thought.

'I wasn't the man Evie needed me to be. She said she couldn't be with me and I understood why she felt that way but I never put up a fight. Yes, we argued, and I told her I would do anything to be with her but … in the end I just left. I didn't even try to find another way because I thought maybe that would make things worse, but for the rest of my life I wished that I had done … *something*.' Vincent felt the anvil that was all tangled up in his heartstrings pull downwards. Lieffe took hold of Vincent's arms.

'You're a good man, Vincent, and Evie continued

7

to love you all her life too. But her life is over now and, well, maybe I shouldn't tell you this ...' He stared intently at Vincent for a moment and Vincent thought his eyes might pop out of his head until he finally blinked and said, 'Oh, never mind. At the moment you're both fighting to find each other. In fact, I'm in there with her, right now.' Lieffe pointed back to Evie's apartment building.

'Eh?' Vincent said, entirely lost.

'This world has a wonderful way of making sure I am where I need to be. Even if that means there's two of me. I wish the real world had worked that way. I'd have got so much more done!' Lieffe chuckled, holding his belly. 'I'm a little bit like the doorman between life and thereafter. I can only show you where to go but if you want to get into your heaven, you've got to find the keys yourself.' Lieffe turned to face Vincent again. 'You didn't feel worthy of her in life because you didn't fight?' Vincent nodded. 'Well, now is your chance to prove you're worthy in the afterlife, it seems.'

Vincent smiled. 'That's all I've ever wanted.'

'Ready, then?' Lieffe asked.

'Ready.'

In an instant Lieffe clicked his bony fingers and the world went dark.

2

The Pivotal Moment

In the click of a light switch, Vincent could see again and the sight made his stomach plummet through the floor. Teenagers were milling around him dressed in ill-fitting tuxedos and marshmallow-like ball gowns, haphazardly thrown together paper chains hung from the ceiling and half-eaten cupcakes lay discarded on their trays. Vincent scanned the room. It was as it had been in life, except everything seemed a little more warped and exaggerated. Teens were dancing in strange jerky movements and most of their faces were indistinct, smudged out of existence. Everything was tinged in blue light and the edges of Vincent's vision seemed a little blurred.

'This is a memory. This is how I remember it.' Vincent said to himself. *But now that I'm actually here*, he thought, *this isn't what it was like at all*. What Vincent did remember correctly, with a pang in his gut, was the reason they had been here at all that night. He waded through the crowd of kids – far bigger in his memory than it ever had been in real life. As he got closer to the stage there stood Vincent's old roommate, Sonny Shine. Sonny was a stage name, although the stages he'd actually played on were few and far between. Vincent was one of only three people who knew what Sonny's real name was – the other two being his own parents.

'Stupid little princess.' Vincent cocked his head at the familiar voice. Standing just a little in front of him in the crowd of faceless youths were none other than Terry Lark and Harrison Feather, Evie's old colleagues at *The Teller*, the newspaper she had worked for when they met. The men stood together with their heads bowed, sniggering and pointing at a figure a few rows in front of them. Vincent followed their oddly elongated fingers and he saw the bouncing curls of a woman shaking her head in embarrassment at Sonny bumbling around on stage. Vincent tried to move towards her but the lights flickered and an electric shock staggered through him. He groaned. He tried once more and the same happened again. It seemed that he had to fight for Evie in a different way than simply through a crowd.

'Ah! The Princess' jester has arrived!' Terry Lark turned to Vincent but his features were twisted. His brows dived dramatically towards the bridge of his spiked nose and his eyes glinted red as the light caught them.

'How much does she pay you to put up with her, Jester?' Harrison's face had elongated downwards and his teeth protruded over his bottom lip like a horse. Vincent could feel his fingers twitch into fists.

'He's probably got a key to the family vault and he's allowed to take as much as he wants. It's not like Princess will miss it!' Terry cackled.

'That depends on how many other men she's coaxed into tending to her every need!' Harrison brayed.

'Nah. No one's stupid enough to fall for her "innocence"', Terry air-quoted with spiked nails. 'She claims she wants to work for herself but then swans off to her apartment paid for by dear old daddy while the rest of us barely make a living.'

11

'No one's stupid enough to fall for it, eh?' Harrison nodded at Vincent whose knuckles were white.

'Ahh, of course. Sorry, mate,' said Terry. 'Guess there is one person just that stu—' Vincent's fist connected with Terry's face for a second time in his memory. There was the *thwack* of skin against skin, the crack of Terry's jaw and the click of Harrison's camera as the front page photo was taken. The flash was like lightning through the hall and an almighty volt of electricity bolted through Vincent's body. He just caught the sad eyes of the curly-haired woman as she turned her head before the room went black.

Vincent panicked, not being able to see, with his hand throbbing and his back against the cold floor of the hall. Just as he was about to scramble up to try to find an escape, the lights crackled back into life. Everything was as it had been. The kids, the decorations, Sonny, the woman, Harrison and an unharmed Terry. Like in a video game, he had failed a level but everything had been reset.

'Ah! The Princess' jester! Is she climbing your tower tonight?'

In a disconcerting loop, Vincent recalled the first time Terry had said that. Everything looked almost the same as before, but even further exaggerated. Terry's

12

and Harrison's faces had never been so demonic. Vincent's memory had warped with age, like a faded photograph where the ink had run. Vincent pulled himself off the floor to face them again.

'Ah, he'll do whatever she says. She's got him under her dainty little thumb,' Harrison sneered.

'Yeah, he's trained up like her little lap dog. Ruff. Ruff. Ruff, ruff!' Terry snarled and barked whilst Harrison howled with laughter. 'Ruff! Ruff! Ru—' Terry was out cold before he could get out another bark. The lights faded once more.

Vincent couldn't help himself. Every time the scene replayed, Terry kept being disgusting, Vincent kept hitting him. After each punch, Vincent was electrocuted – and yet he never felt all that sorry.

'You know you're probably one of many men she's playing with, don't yo—' *Bang. Zap.*

'Tell me, Jester. She's innocent when she's out of the house but she's filthy in bed, isn't sh—' *Thud. Zap.*

'Girls like her always get their own way! Always playing games. Prissy little bitc—' *Whack. Zap.*

Terry didn't know how to keep his mouth shut and Vincent didn't know any other way of silencing him.

The school hall lights came on again and Vincent scanned the crowd for Evie's hair but this time she had disappeared. He thought back to the real night of this distorted replication he was being forced to live over and over again. He had punched Terry, Harrison had taken a picture that ended up on the front page of *The Teller* and Evie's foul mother, Eleanor, had seen it. Eleanor Snow had been embarrassed by Evie's desire to work as well as her dream of becoming an artist. Eleanor had wanted her daughter to stay at home, marry the man Eleanor had chosen for her and provide her with grandchildren, which was eventually just what Evie had done. However, Evie had put up a fight and demanded that her mother must at least give her a chance to live the life she wanted to live so, reluctantly, Eleanor had agreed. However, there was a caveat: had Evie not progressed in her field within the year, she was to come home. Evie found herself a job as a cartoonist but Vincent's actions on the night he was reliving had cost Evie her job – they hadn't known it then but it had been the beginning of the end.

Vincent had thought he was defending Evie's honour by hitting Terry in his foul mouth but the fact that he'd spent the rest of his life wishing he'd fought for her harder, better, proved that on this night, he hadn't been defending Evie at all. Not in a way that was actually helpful at least. This was the pivotal moment.

Now's my chance, he thought, as the memory repeated once again.

'Ah! The Princess' jester has arrived! She'll be delighted to see her lapdog!'

'Maybe she'll give you a bone,' Harrison sniggered.

'Or maybe he'll give *her* one!' They laughed.

'LISTEN.' Vincent raised his voice, his anger needing to bubble over in some way. He breathed deeply. 'That's *enough*, Terry. She's worth a million of you. A million of both of you.' Terry snorted but didn't retort. 'You've made her a princess in your heads because neither of you have any other way to justify your jealousy and bitterness.'

'Jealous? Of that little brat?' Harrison sneered.

'Mate. C'mon. You only call her Princess because she's got more money than you. She's never given you any other reason for that nickname so if it's not coming from jealousy, where's it coming from, eh?'

Terry huffed but remained silent.

'Neither of you have bothered to get to know Evie because it's easier to hate this idea you've created than it is to know the real person. Why don't you let go of how you feel and admit that maybe, you're wrong.'

Harrison played with the buttons on his camera, avoiding Vincent's gaze.

'She wasn't perfect and she came from a completely different world than you, than all of us. Which means you may not have had a lot in common with her but that doesn't mean she deserved the shit you put her through. And she never once batted an eyelid at the things you said, never rose to the bait, never said an unkind word about either of you, all of that goes to show that she was and always will be better than the both of you, better than all of us.'

It took everything Vincent had to turn and walk away without breaking anything (including Terry's nose) but a warm feeling rose up from his heart and out through his veins. He was *proud* of himself.

'Vincent.'

'Evie?' Vincent spun around to see Evie's face in the crowd and although she was blurred, her features smudged, he could tell that she was smiling. Then the world fell away again.

3

The Hopeless House

Vincent walked through darkness until the black faded to grey then the grey merged into blue and walls started to form around him. He continued down what emerged as a long corridor and saw paintings and mirrors materialise around him. At the end of the corridor Vincent saw a black door with a large silver knocker in the shape of a squirrel's tail. The walls squirmed and rippled, causing panic to rise in Vincent's chest, but as he finally stumbled to the door, he began to feel calmer. The silver squirrel's tail curved satisfying against his palm and he swung it against the door fast, three times. *Knock, knock, knock.*

'Come in,' said a small voice.

Vincent couldn't see a doorknob so he pushed against the wood, but the door wouldn't budge. He strained his shoulder against it and the hinges gave a soft creak. Then, he slammed his weight against the door and it finally cracked open, black paint chips and wood splintering into the air. Vincent still had to kick the bottom of the door with the heel of his boot to open enough of a gap to get through.

The room on the other side was grey like the corridor but the fireplace in the corner brought a welcome burst of colour and warmth. The two armchairs either side of the fire looked comfortable and inviting. Once inside, brushing the wood from his coat, Vincent noticed small white spots appearing on the black of his sleeve. Holding the fabric closer to his eyes he realised they weren't appearing, but landing. It was snowing. Only faintly, with the flakes melting on impact, but it was most certainly snowing. Cold and crisp.

'Snow.' He smiled.

'I'd prefer it if you called me Eleanor.' That voice again. Weak and tinged with sadness, it was coming from one of the armchairs. Vincent let his eyes adjust to the dark for a moment before replying.

'Eleanor? You're Evie's mother?' He stood, stock still.

'*Evie*,' she whispered.

Vincent could now see her silhouette against the flames, small and fragile, her lips pursed. He walked towards her slowly.

'I—' He began to speak before realising he didn't know what he wanted to say. 'Why am I *here*?'

'Probably because my daughter can't let you go.' Eleanor rolled her eyes. She was in a formal grey suit but it looked faded, washed out, as though it was once a different colour. Her skin was only a shade lighter than her suit, her hair was white and her eyes were black. Vincent saw that she was sitting in a puddle of pale blue, like someone had spilt a whole can of paint on the grey armchair. She was entirely drained of colour.

'Then the feeling's mutual,' Vincent said.

'Hmm.' She eyed him, taking him in for the first time. 'Seems that way. Why else would you be here?' Vincent gestured questioningly to the armchair and she nodded so he sat, uncomfortably adjusting himself several times before settling.

'I don't actually know why I'm here.' *Of all places, why am I here?* He cursed whoever or whatever force had brought him face to face with a woman he disliked without ever having met. He looked around, hoping to spot a clue that would tell him why the universe

19

wanted him to speak to Eleanor Snow, of all people. *I wonder if this is hell after all,* he thought.

'Neither do I. I've been stuck here ever since I died and no matter what I do, the corridors of this house always lead me back to this room.' Eleanor flung herself out of her seat sharply and started pacing, her gaze drifting from wall to wall. 'I'm not sure I'll ever leave,' she whimpered.

This was the first time Vincent had met Evie's mother and from what he knew of her, she was cold and unfriendly. Although the woman in front of him seemed both of those things, there was also a tinge of vulnerability in her that Evie had never mentioned. Either it had been there all along and well hidden, or it had developed during Eleanor's time in this strange house.

'Mrs Snow?' Vincent asked but Eleanor remained focused on the room. 'Why did you treat your daughter the way you did?'

Eleanor's head whipped round at him.

'*Excuse me?*' she spat.

'I'm sorry, I just—'

'I knew my daughter better than you ever did in that year you two … *shacked up.* I knew her and I knew what was good for her and I would have gotten my way had you not interfered!' She pointed a bony finger at him with force.

'You *did* get your way. She married the man you had chosen for her.' Vincent felt his stomach churn with upset and frustration.

'But she wasn't *happy* about it.' Eleanor let out a sob before she turned away. Vincent heard her breathe deeply, composing herself. 'I didn't want her to work because she didn't need to. We had everything in the world in this house.' She gestured to the walls and Vincent realised he was sitting in the Snows' living room, that this was the house Evie had grown up in. Suddenly, he felt it was a less cold and unfriendly place to be. 'No worrying about the next pay cheque or the next meal,' Eleanor went on. 'She even had a good-looking man from a respectable family who loved her, who was willing to be hers for ever. She had everything, but was she grateful? Of *course* not.'

'Evie wanted to be independent.' Vincent said. 'She was twenty-seven, not seventeen, but you tried to make all the decisions for her, like she was a child. Anyone would feel suffocated and I'm surprised she didn't crack sooner.'

'The way she acted was ridiculous! Having everything wasn't enough if she hadn't got those things for herself. She was too proud, too stupid and too selfish—'

'Too selfish?' Vincent said. 'Too *selfish*? Evie gave up everything she'd ever wanted because of you, because of the way you treated her – and don't get me started on the way you treated Eddie.' Vincent sat forwards in his armchair. The anger was bubbling through his blood but he was careful not to lose his temper.

'Eddie ...?' she said.

'You would have disowned him because of his sexuality and Evie wouldn't have been able to support him if she'd stayed with me. We would have had no money and potentially no roof over our heads and that was OK with her – we would have managed somehow, just the two of us. But when she found out Eddie's secret ... she had no choice but to marry Jim. She needed to be able to look after her brother, independently.'

A gust of wind blew more snow down onto Vincent. The flakes were larger and colder than before, and they didn't melt as soon as they landed.

'No ... I ...' Eleanor stuttered.

'She needed to marry into money and stability in order to give Eddie the life he eventually had because

Lord knows what would have happened to him had he stayed with you.'

'HE WOULD HAVE BEEN HAPPY!' Eleanor screamed.

The walls warped, stretching the room. The fireplace opened, mimicking Eleanor's mouth, and roared, the flames licking at the edges of the hearth like a tongue. The heat and ferocity sent Vincent tumbling out of his chair, cowering under the collar of his coat to protect his face. Eleanor exhaled and the room calmed instantly, returning to its usual shape, but the wallpaper was now severely torn and scorched leaving eerie, jagged gaps.

'Eddie would have been fine. He was my son and I loved him.' Eleanor made her way to the other armchair, shakily easing herself into it. 'My husband didn't understand and never would have but I—' She sobbed again. 'I would have kept him safe. He was my boy. I would have made sure he was all right.'

Vincent felt his heart ache. If what Eleanor was saying was true, then Eddie would have been OK after all. It was so hard for him to know that Evie could have stayed with him, that they could have built a life together. But she couldn't have taken that risk – she didn't trust her mother. Vincent understood that but it didn't make it any easier to know.

'I never saw my son after the night he ran away. I always hoped—' Eleanor sniffed, '—but I never did.'

'You could have called him, you could have written letters. Visited Evie and Jim. Anything!' Vincent said, standing up again. 'Anything to let Eddie know you were there for him.'

'I KNOW!' Eleanor shook as she spoke. '*I wish I had*,' she whispered and Vincent wondered if that was what was keeping her here. Her guilt. 'I just want to see him again.'

'Judging by the way he looked when I saw him last, you may be waiting a long time.' Vincent remembered Eddie's cheeky face and the way he gazed at his husband, Oliver. He was an old man back in the land of the living but he had a good few years in him yet, of that Vincent was sure.

'You knew my son?' Her black eyes glinted in the light of the flames.

'I only met him the once but he's well.' Vincent smiled.

'And happy?' She smiled back through tears at Vincent's nod.

To Vincent, the Eleanor that had once existed was merely a hardened shell around a soft centre. So she *did* have a heart after all – it seemed there was so much

24

more going on inside that no one had ever known about. It may have been small, but it was there and it was working. Vincent wondered if this might be his chance.

'Eleanor.' She didn't look up as she wiped at her tears but appeared to be listening. 'I loved your daughter. More than anything on Earth. Had she stayed with me, we may not have had anything to call our own but we would have had each other. Your obsession with money, connections and stability were old-fashioned, overrated and cost your daughter her life's happiness.' Vincent paused. He thought he'd heard Eleanor whisper, '*I know*,' but he wasn't sure, so he continued. 'I made mistakes in my lifetime but I would have given your daughter the moon if I could have. Hell, I would have thrown in the stars as well!' Eleanor smiled into her lap. 'But I was never given that chance and just like you didn't fight for Eddie, I didn't fight for Evie and that's why I'm here.' Vincent shivered. The snow had started to come down heavily and was collecting on his coat and chair.

'Jim made her happy, though,' Eleanor said, frowning.

'Eventually. Mainly through the children they raised, but he wasn't what she wanted. The life you and he gave her wasn't the one she wanted. She made the best out of a bad situation because that's what Evie did. But I want you to know that we're both here in this world now, fighting to be with each other once more. We will get the happy ending we should have had. The happy ending you took away from us.' Vincent couldn't stop talking. It was as if a tiny pin had pricked his heart and all the things he'd wanted to say to Eleanor Snow were slowly leaking out, word by word. Eleanor didn't flinch at his harsh words.

'I know,' she said. 'But I'm not sorry. I believe I was doing the right thing for my daughter and I had to see it through. Eventually she got everything she deserved.'

'But not what she wanted.' Vincent clenched his fists, his nails digging into his palms.

'Sometimes a mother knows best.' Her lips were pursed again, the hard exterior reforming.

'Sometimes, Eleanor, she doesn't,' he said, sweating.

Eleanor looked at Vincent but this time, she *saw* him too. She noticed the warmth in his eyes and her heart softened.

'But,' she said, 'I am glad you'll find each other again this side of life. I'm … I'm glad she'll finally get what she wanted.' Eleanor shrugged.

'So am I.'

26

At her words a gust of wind whipped up the snow on the floor. The snow spiraled into a small hurricane, then unravelled and straightened into a thin line. It swirled its way to the far side of the room where a black hole had appeared. Vincent thought maybe his brain was playing tricks on him but he was certain he could hear the steady rhythm of trains barrelling past on their tracks.

'I think that's your cue,' Eleanor said without looking at the tunnel. She knew it wasn't for her. 'She's probably waiting.'

'She won't be for much longer,' Vincent said as the snow twisted around his legs, rope-like, and started to pull him towards the black hole. Just as he found the courage to move forward, Eleanor snatched his hand.

'Tell her ... I'm sorry, will you?'

Vincent wondered if she really meant it but when he looked down at her in her armchair, he noticed to his surprise her eyes had turned blue and he nodded. Then he let the snow carry him into the tunnel and he was encompassed by darkness again.

4

Evie's Song

Reaching solid ground Vincent started walking and continued for what seemed like miles. He could feel the floor under his boots turn from carpet to hard, tiled floor. A light up ahead started to materialise and the snow became more frantic the closer he got. It was only when he was close enough to make out the platform signs of a familiar train station in the distance that the snow stopped abruptly in the air, frozen in place. Vincent waved his hand against it like he was opening a curtain and the snow that touched his palm fell away. The snow had been its own entity, keeping him company on the long walk and now it was inanimate, he felt a sense of loneliness in the last few minutes it took to reach the train station.

Vincent found himself in front of the old busking spot he'd occupied for many years. It was the place he'd earned his rent money (barely), the place he'd done his thinking and most importantly, the place he had first met *her*. Vincent could remember exactly how Evie had looked when he'd opened his eyes and seen her standing in front of him for the first time. Her face was so round and all her features were so big, just as she'd drawn them in the picture she'd left in his case the day before. He thought she'd been exaggerating and was, perhaps, being funny but really, she'd been quite accurate. But it wasn't really the way she looked that had got his attention. It was her *twinkle*. Although he thought Evie was pretty, had she not had that spark, he wouldn't have been half as interested. It was the life in her eyes when she talked about things she loved and the slight twitch of her lips when she knew she shouldn't be smiling. Evie Snow looked like she was laughing even when she wasn't and when he woke up to her still-dreaming face, he had said it was like waking up with sunshine. It was that very twinkle that Vincent fell in love with because he'd never seen anyone wear it as well as she did.

Vincent's black violin was in its case in his usual spot. Gently, he crouched, lifted it onto his lap and flipped the latches. Holding his violin again was something he was sure he wouldn't be able to do now that he was dead. A tear ran down his cheek as he pressed his chin into the rest and the bow gently touched the strings. As he played the first long note, an icy air brushed across his closed eyelids. He stopped playing, opened his eyes and noticed there was fresh snow settling by his feet. He played one staccato note, this time watching as the snow jumped at the sound. He played a few more stabs and the snowflakes danced. Vincent laughed and played another long note. The snow lifted into the air but this time Vincent kept playing. Each beautiful, heartfelt note had the snowflakes twirling and dancing, and carefully they came together to form a river of snow once more.

Vincent watched in awe as he played, though faltered in panic as the snow found its way under his feet and began to lift him. He tried to move out of its way but it was far stronger than he was expecting and he was no match for it. The snow wrapped around his legs and when he was three inches, four inches, five inches off the ground, he stopped resisting. Vincent closed his eyes, gave in to the snow, and simply played.

31

Slowly, he was carried through the station. The more love he put into the melodies, the faster he floated.

Vincent was playing a beautiful tune he'd written a long time ago, for Evie. A waltz he'd never had the chance to play for her or dance with her to. The song stirred and excited the snow and it carried him up the steps of the station and out into the world, past houses and bridges and the place they shared their first kiss. Vincent's bow glided across the strings and he let himself laugh as he felt himself getting lighter and lighter. The snowflakes were taking every ounce of his weight; he felt like he was flying. He spun through the icy air and wherever he placed his feet, the snow found him and never let him fall. More and more snow fell and joined in his dance until he was in the centre of a blizzard and had he opened his eyes, he wouldn't have been able to see his own violin.

Vincent was playing the last few bars of his song. He opened his eyes momentarily and through his eyelashes he saw the balcony of Evie's flat at the end of the lane. His song had been carrying him right to her and now that she was within reach, he squeezed his eyes shut tightly and played harder than ever before. Although his fingers were numb and his skin was red raw, he had to see her, if only for a moment. He felt himself spiral up and up, seven stories high, the snow guiding his feet up invisible steps. As Vincent ran his bow over the strings for the last time, the snow calmed, lowered him gently downwards and on the final note, his feet touched the stone paving of the balcony floor. He opened his eyes and looked over the railings to see every inch of the street below covered in a crisp, freshly fallen, white blanket. Everything appeared to be frozen, blissfully still.

Evie's flat had never officially been his home. He'd only ever stayed over for days at a time and their story hadn't even lasted a year, but it was the place he had always felt he belonged the most. Wherever Evie was felt like home to him. Vincent felt a chill in his bones, partly from the wintery scene below him, but mostly because this was the last place he'd seen Evie. It was on this very spot on the balcony where she had told him it had to end. He could hear her voice in his head like it was yesterday.

'*Eddie snuck out in the early hours of the morning the other night and he came here. We talked and he admitted to me … well, he told me was gay. I've sort of known for years but it was the first time he actually said the words to me. He wants to tell Mother and Father the truth, but when he does …*' Evie paused,

'Mother will throw him out. He'll be alone, so I need to take care of him.'

'Right.' Vincent had said.

'If we run away, if I'm not there to help him, he'll carry on pretending he's something he's not because he'll have nowhere else to go. He can't live like that. If I stay, I'll have to marry Jim … but that means I could look after Eddie. I could give him a place to stay and the life he deserves, and Mother would never have to know.'

Vincent had listened in silence and wondered when something so simple had turned into something so impossible. He'd cursed the universe for years for dealing him a hand in which the only woman he'd ever wanted to give his heart to had found herself in a situation where choosing Vincent was a risk she couldn't take. In almost every way they had been a perfect match and yet they'd missed out on their happy ending. Vincent wondered how many people got the chance he was being given now, the chance to be with the one that got away. How many couples miss their chance in life but find themselves together in a world beyond the living? Vincent silently wished them all happy final adventures together, wherever they were.

Vincent turned to the balcony doors and went to twist the handle but it stuck in his hand. He rattled it but it wouldn't budge.

'What more do I have to prove?' He sighed, leaning his head against the glass pane. 'I've fought for you, Evie. I've pushed against hurricanes. I've controlled my temper and used words instead of fists. I've stood up to your terrifyingly unstable mother and I've played until my fingers were numb.' He caught himself before a sob could escape. 'What more can I do for you, Evie? Tell me and I'll do it.'

'It's not always about you, you whiny git!' a voice from below yelled, cracking the stillness of the snow. Vincent knew that voice but it sounded much younger than he'd ever heard it before. He turned to the railings and leant over to see a teenage boy with ruffled blond hair, gangly limbs and drumsticks hanging out of his back pocket.

'Sonny?' Vincent's breath caught in his throat. Sonny Shine had drunk himself into an early grave around the age of fifty-four and although Vincent had warned him a thousand times and his death hadn't come as much of a surprise, Vincent's heart had still broken when he heard of Sonny's passing. He was the only real friend he'd ever had, the kind of friend you love like a brother, even though they irritate you all the time.

'It's Edgar, actually.' Young Sonny smiled sheepishly.

'Edgar? You always hated that name. You said you'd kill me if I ever told anyone that time I saw it on your driving licence. Remember? When they confiscated it because you hadn't paid your many, *many* parking fines?' Vincent shook his head, remembering the various scrapes Sonny had got them both into.

'Yeah, I know, but I'm fourteen here. Before Sonny Shine even existed. Before things got ... y'know ... shit.'

'Hey. You're fourteen. You can't say shit— I mean, stuff like that.' Vincent laughed at the strangeness of seeing someone he knew so well so young and innocent. Sonny hadn't been innocent in any way; Edgar seemed to be.

'I know. My mum hates it. It seems I was happiest before I was Sonny, back when I was Edgar Cloude and living off of my mum's homemade cottage pie. Mate, you've gotta come over and try it.' Edgar smiled broadly.

'I'd love to, Sonny ... sorry, Edgar.'

'Hey! Is Evie up there?! Bring her too!' Edgar jumped up and down, trying to see past Vincent.

'No, she isn't, but … I'm hoping maybe she will be soon.' He looked back at the doors. They were still firmly shut.

'Well, I have to get back to Mum but I'm so glad you're here. Well, I'm not glad you're dead. Just … here.' Edgar laughed, waved and ran through the snow leaving hefty boot prints behind him and Vincent felt his heart swell, knowing his friend was happy and safe.

Vincent heard an odd scratching noise behind him. He spun around, hoping the doors had opened, but instead he was greeted with a bird, white and silky, perched on the door handle. He cooed softly and bowed his head.

'Little One?' Vincent's eyes welled up and he knelt by the bird's side and waggled a finger under his chin. 'It's so good to see you.'

Little One looked over his shoulder through the window and flapped his wings, flying over to the railings, as though he was getting out of the way. It was then that Vincent noticed someone had entered the flat. His heart started thudding hard. He could feel his pulse in the tip of every finger, hear it booming in his ears. Looking through the windows, he could see the silhouette of a woman wearing a coat. She seemed to be looking at him too.

Vincent lifted his trembling hand and took hold of the handle. He turned it and this time it moved, and he felt the latch click open. Vincent couldn't bring himself to open the door all at once. Crazy thoughts started to run through his head. *What if this is the wrong flat?* he thought. *What if that's not Evie? What if this is all a dream brought on by eating weird fruit from a weird tree?*

Whatever was happening, he need to know for sure. He took a breath and pushed open the door ... and there she was. Green coat, blonde hair, and that twinkle. *That twinkle.* He stepped into the room and before he'd even taken a breath, she was running to him. Opening his arms, she ran into them at full tilt and he swept her up gladly. Vincent couldn't believe this was real, that *she* was real. He held her tight against him and the smell of treacle enveloped him. He took her face in his calloused hands and stroked her cheeks with his thumbs.

Evie Snow found his green eyes and that was all it took to convince him this wasn't a dream. She was here and she was real.

Evie ran her fingers through his hair, not able to get enough of him after half a century without him. Vincent moved his lips to hers, and just before he kissed her, Evie whispered, 'At long last.'

Epilogue

The Greatest Adventure

Reunited, they found the sofa and unmoving, just silent, they held each other for what seemed like forever and yet it still didn't feel like long enough. This was something they had both spent half a century longing for and now that they had it, they couldn't believe it was real. Evie's hands had locked themselves in Vincent's hair, her legs over his lap and even though her palms were sweating, she couldn't let him go. Vincent cradled her and squeezed her every once in a while, to reassure her he was still there and always would be. They really did have each other once more.

After a while, Vincent felt Evie shudder and realised she was crying.

'Hey. What's wrong?' He pulled away so he could look into her face.

'Nothing's wrong.' She shook her head, smiling. 'I'm happy. So, *unbelievably* happy but I'm also … confused. This feels like a dream but it also feels real but we're both dead so … how *can* it be real?' Evie wiped her eyes on the sleeve of her green coat.

Vincent shrugged. 'I don't know. Maybe it's best not to overthink something as unexplained and complicated as the afterlife.' He chuckled.

'I guess so,' she said. She looked at him. 'I lived a whole life without you. I had children. With someone else. Now I'm back with you, back in this time, I've got a chance to do what I wanted to do with no boundaries but is it real if it isn't … *life*?'

'Does it matter?' Vincent asked, taking Evie's wringing hands. 'Does it matter if it's real or not if you're happy?'

Evie thought for a moment. 'I guess not. It's just a shame.' She looked at their clasped hands.

'We know it's a shame we never got the happy ending we should have had in life but … we're together now. That's what matters the most, isn't it?' Vincent said, stroking the side of her face.

Evie nodded and her face burst into the most glorious smile Vincent had ever seen and she happily snuggled into him once more.

'So what now?' Evie asked.

Vincent chuckled and said ...

'We *live*.'

Carrie Hope Fletcher is an actress, singer, vlogger and, thanks to her popular YouTube channel ItsWayPastMyBedTime, 'honorary big sister' to hundreds of thousands of young people around the world. Carrie's first book, *All I Know Now*, was a number one *Sunday Times* bestseller and her debut novel, *On the Other Side*, also went straight to number one in its first week on sale.

Carrie has played the role of Eponine in *Les Misérables* at the Queen's Theatre in London's West End and received the 2014 WhatsOnStage Award for Best Takeover in a Role. In 2016 she starred as Truly Scrumptious in the UK tour of *Chitty Chitty Bang Bang*. Carrie lives just outside London with numerous fictional friends that she keeps on bookshelves, just in case.

www.youtube.com/carrie
@CarrieHFletcher

Read *On the Other Side*,
the debut novel and *Sunday Times*
number one bestseller from

Carrie Hope Fletcher

Evie Snow is eighty-two when she quietly passes away but when she reaches the door of her own private heaven, she finds that she's become her twenty-seven-year-old self and the door won't open. She soon learns that she must unburden her soul of the three secrets which have weighed her down for over fifty years before she can pass over, so she must find a way to reveal them before it's too late. As Evie begins the journey of a lifetime, somehow, some way, she may also find her way back to the only man she ever truly loved …

Powerful, magical and utterly romantic, *On the Other Side* is a love story like no other and will transport you to a world that is impossible to forget.

'Spellbinding'
Miranda Dickinson

AVAILABLE NOW!